Contents

KU-031-722

SKATER'S
SECRET

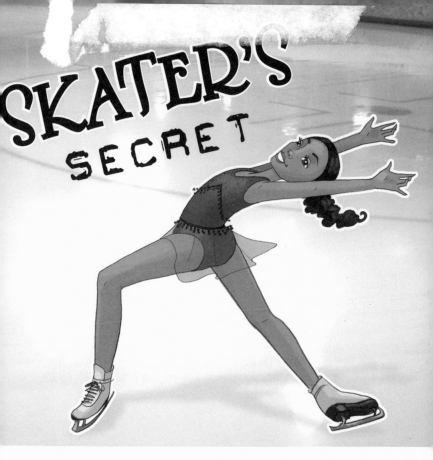

Lisa Trumbauer

illustrated by Tuesday Mourning

www.raintreepublishers.co.uk
Visit our website to find out
more information about
Raintree books.

To order:
☎ Phone 0845 6044371
🖨 Fax +44 (0) 1865 312263
💻 Email myorders@capstonepub.co.uk

Customers from outside the UK please telephone +44 1865 312262

Raintree is an imprint of Capstone Global Library Limited, a company incorporated in England and Wales having its registered office at 7 Pilgrim Street, London, EC4V 6LB – Registered company number: 6695582

"Raintree" is a registered trademark of Pearson Education Limited, under licence to Capstone Global Library Limited

Text © Stone Arch Books 2010
First published by Stone Arch Books in 2010
First published in hardback and paperback in the United Kingdom by
Capstone Global Library in 2010
The moral rights of the proprietor have been asserted.

All rights reserved. No part of this publication may be reproduced in any form or by any means (including photocopying or storing it in any medium by electronic means and whether or not transiently or incidentally to some other use of this publication) without the written permission of the copyright owner, except in accordance with the provisions of the Copyright, Designs and Patents Act 1988 or under the terms of a licence issued by the Copyright Licensing Agency, Saffron House, 6–10 Kirby Street, London EC1N 8TS (www.cla.co.uk). Applications for the copyright owner's written permission should be addressed to the publisher.

Edited in the United Kingdom by Diyan Leake
Original illustrations © Stone Arch Books 2010
Illustrated by Tuesday Mourning
Originated by Capstone Global Library Ltd
Printed in China by Leo Paper Products Ltd

ISBN 978 1 406 21387 4 (hardback)
14 13 12 11 10
10 9 8 7 6 5 4 3 2 1

ISBN 978 1 406 21408 6 (paperback)
14 13 12 11 10
10 9 8 7 6 5 4 3 2 1

British Library Cataloguing in Publication Data
Trumbauer, Lisa – Skater's secret
A full catalogue record for this book is available from the British Library.

Acknowledgements
We would like to thank the following for permission to reproduce photographs: Shutterstock Images/Close Encounters Photography cover (background)

Every effort has been made to contact copyright holders of material reproduced in this book. Any omissions will be rectified in subsequent printings if notice is given to the publisher.

Disclaimer
All the Internet addresses (URLs) given in this book were valid at the time of going to press. However, due to the dynamic nature of the Internet, some addresses may have changed, or sites may have changed or ceased to exist since publication. While the author and publisher regret any inconvenience this may cause readers, no responsibility for any such changes can be accepted by either the author or the publisher.

 # The Secret

Standing by the rail of the skating rink, Maggie watched the skater on the ice.

The skater moved with grace. She sailed across the ice effortlessly. One arm was raised in front of her body. Her other arm curled towards her back.

She lifted her chin proudly, and a small smile tugged at her mouth.

Maggie sighed. The skater was so perfect.

Okay, so she was a few years older than Maggie. Two years, to be exact. She'd had two more years to perfect her style and movements. Maggie still had time to be as good as her sister.

Still, Maggie couldn't help but be jealous.

"Your sister looks great out there," Maggie's best friend, Elly, said.

Maggie sighed. "Shannon always looks great," she said.

"You don't sound very happy about that," Elly said.

"I just wish she wasn't so great, you know?" Maggie said quietly.

Elly nudged Maggie playfully on the shoulder. "Oh, come on. You're a great skater too," Elly said, smiling.

Maggie tried to smile back. "I never feel great when Shannon's around," she admitted.

Elly shook her head. "Don't be silly," she said. "You skate as well as Shannon. Your skating is just different."

Maggie turned to face Elly. "Different? How?" she asked.

"Well, your skating is more athletic," Elly explained. "Look. Watch Shannon."

Maggie turned back to the ice. Her sister had begun to speed around the rink, her arms waving behind her. The short skirt of her light-blue practice outfit looked like flower petals. She shifted slowly, and her skates turned around. Shannon continued to skate, but now she skated backwards. She raised her arms over her head.

"Okay, so?" Maggie asked Elly. "What are you trying to show me?"

"Well, if you were doing this routine, you would have leaped into a twirl or something fantastic by now," Elly explained. "Shannon is a great skater, but she just keeps skating straight."

"Does that make me a better skater?" Maggie asked.

"It makes you a different skater," Elly said.

Maggie rested her elbow on the rink's rail. She propped her chin in her raised hand. "I don't want to be different. I want to skate like that," she said, looking at her sister.

Maggie and Elly continued to watch Shannon on the ice.

Shannon skated a few more laps around the rink. She never stumbled or seemed unsure.

Maggie admired her sister. She admired her sister's talent and ability, and she admired how much Shannon loved skating. But she didn't admire how Shannon always did better than she did during competitions.

"The next competition is in three weeks, right?" Maggie asked.

"Yep," Elly said. "I've been working with my coach on a great routine."

"That's the problem," Maggie said, sighing. "Shannon and I share a coach."

"So what?" Elly asked.

"So I don't want Shannon to know what my routine is," Maggie explained.

"Then ask your coach not to tell her," Elly said.

Maggie was silent. Then she said, "Maybe I'll keep my routine a secret from both of them."

 Older Sisters

Later that day, Maggie sat on the purple rug in her room. She closed her eyes and listened to the music coming through her headphones. She tried to picture herself skating to the music.

She didn't notice when Shannon walked in. Shannon tapped her shoulder, and Maggie jumped.

"What are you doing in my room?" Maggie asked.

"I knocked, but you didn't hear me," Shannon said.

"I was just listening to music," Maggie told her.

"Obviously. You're listening pretty hard," Shannon said.

Maggie shrugged, trying to act like it was no big deal. "I'm just thinking," she said.

"Just thinking, huh?" Shannon said doubtfully. "I have the feeling you're looking for a song for our next skating competition."

Maggie crossed her arms. "Maybe I am," she said. "What are you skating to?"

"I don't know yet," Shannon admitted. "I'm working on it with my coach. He keeps playing me stuff that I don't like."

She flopped on Maggie's bed. Leaning up on one elbow, Shannon looked down to where Maggie sat on the floor.

Shannon said, "I do want to use a classical piece, though. I know the judges like classical music. And I know classical music shows off my skating."

Maggie shrugged again. "Yeah, I guess," she said.

"And I'm trying to move up from novice to junior, too," Shannon went on.

Maggie jerked her head up. She knew she shouldn't be surprised. Shannon had been on the novice level for at least a year. At 15, she was definitely ready to move up to the junior level. That meant that Shannon would be leaving Maggie behind again.

Maggie sighed. Shannon was definitely going to breeze through the junior level, just like she breezed through everything else. All that was left after that was the senior level. The best skaters in the world were seniors.

Maggie turned around to look at her sister. "I'm sure you'll find the perfect song," she told Shannon. "And I'm sure you'll make junior level, no problem."

Shannon sat up and smiled. She asked, "Do you really think so?"

"Sure," Maggie said. "You get everything else you try for, don't you?"

"Hardly!" Shannon said. She got up and added, "By the way, Mum said to tell you that dinner's almost ready." With a toss of her hair, she strolled out of the bedroom.

Maggie was usually happy being twelve years old. She didn't mind being the younger sister.

Right then, though, she wished she could be the older sister. Just once.

Found It!

The next day after school, Maggie, Elly, and Shannon had ballet class. The class was for skaters to learn to move gracefully.

The ballet teacher, Mrs Harris, showed them how to wave their arms so they looked like tree limbs, blowing in the wind. She taught them how to hold their heads and how to stand up straight. She also taught them how to twirl and how to position their legs.

let classes were really hard. Maggie never felt free during ballet classes.

When she was on the ice, she soared. She felt wonderful. The cool air from the rink blew across her face. It flowed through her curls. Moving her legs pushed her forwards quickly. She loved every minute of being on the ice.

Being stuck in the dance studio was awful. In dance class, Maggie's body felt silly and lumpy. The black leotard clung to her body in weird ways. She always felt like a duck with two giant feet and not enough feathers.

Mrs Harris directed the girls to bend one leg and twirl across the dance floor. Shannon took the lead, and the rest of the class followed.

"Smoother, Maggie!" Mrs Harris called across the studio. "And stand up straight!"

Maggie felt heat rush up her face. That was another reason why she and ballet classes did not go together. Mrs Harris was always pointing out her mistakes.

Maggie did what she was told. She straightened her shoulders. She held her head up high. She flung her arms out beside her.

She spun and spun and spun and spun. Then she crashed right into Elly.

"Pay attention!" Mrs Harris said. She clapped her hands twice.

"Sorry," Maggie whispered to Elly.

Elly giggled. "It's not a big deal," she whispered back. "At least class is almost over."

"I know!" Maggie said. "I can't wait."

After class, she and Shannon would head to the rink. There, they would skate for about an hour. Mr Peters would split his time between the two of them.

Maggie always wished she had her own skating instructor, but she knew that good skating instructors were hard to find. The lessons cost a lot of money, too.

Mr Peters was an excellent instructor. Maggie knew she was lucky to be his pupil.

Finally, ballet class ended. Maggie walked over to her gym bag against the wall. She pulled out a purple hoodie and jogging bottoms and slipped them on. Then she walked from the studio with Elly and Shannon.

As they walked through the corridors of the dance school, they passed many rooms full of dancers. Music drifted through the doorways.

In front of one room, a song came through the open doorway. Maggie stopped and looked in. The dancers inside were amazing. The music seemed to flow through them and into their bodies.

As she watched the dancers, Maggie suddenly knew. She knew she'd found it.

This was her song.

Chapter Four

Prepare and Practise

Maggie knew she had to be careful. She didn't want Shannon to know what she was doing.

"Um, I think I see someone I know," Maggie said, thinking fast. "I'll be right back."

Then she ducked into the ballet studio. She didn't wait for Elly or Shannon to reply.

Quietly, Maggie walked around the edge of the room. She didn't want to disturb the dancers. She just wanted the name of the song they were dancing to.

"Excuse me," Maggie said softly to the dance instructor. The instructor kept her gaze focused on her students, but she nodded slightly.

"Could you tell me what this song is called?" Maggie asked quietly.

The teacher continued to study the dancers. "It's the *Moonlight Sonata*," she said. "By Beethoven."

"Thank you!" Maggie whispered. She repeated the title in her mind. She didn't want to write it down. She didn't want Shannon to have any way of finding out the name of the song.

She headed back to the corridor. "Who do you know in that class?" Shannon asked.

Maggie shrugged. "I was wrong. It just looked like a friend of mine," she said. Shannon frowned, but she didn't ask any more questions.

At the skating rink, Maggie enjoyed her hour on the ice. As she skated, the haunting melody of the Beethoven song glided through her mind. She began thinking about a routine to go with the song. She'd need to be able to hear the music for real. Then she could plan her skating routine.

Soon, Shannon's half hour with Mr Peters was over. It was Maggie's turn to work with the coach.

"How are you doing today, Maggie?" Mr Peters asked as he walked up.

"Oh, I'm fine!" Maggie said. And she meant it. She knew her song choice was perfect for her. The slow, gentle song would show off her graceful movements. She'd prove that she could be just as graceful as Shannon.

"Have you picked out a song for your routine yet?" Mr Peters asked.

Maggie hated to lie to her instructor, but she didn't want Shannon to find out what her song was. "Not really," Maggie answered. "I'd like to choose something soft, to show off my more graceful side."

"Graceful is good," Mr Peters said, "but you are such a strong skater. Your music should be strong too."

Maggie frowned. "What do you mean?" she asked. "Are you saying I'm not graceful?"

"Yes, you are graceful," Mr Peters said. "You're also very powerful. Your jumps are wonderful. I'd like to see you work on a combination of jumps."

"A combination? But isn't that usually for the junior skaters?" Maggie asked, confused.

Mr Peters nodded. "Yes, but I think you could be ready," he told her.

"But I've only been at the novice level for a few months," Maggie said.

"We can still prepare and practise," Mr Peters said. He clapped his hands together and said, "Okay. Let's see an Axel, followed by a double toe loop."

The *Moonlight Sonata* left Maggie's head. She pushed off against the ice. She gained speed as she moved around the rink. She thought about the jumps Mr Peters had asked her to do.

At the same time, she thought about her ballet class, and standing straight, and spinning on one foot. A thumping, grinding rhythm raced through her brain.

She was ready.

Leaping upwards, Maggie moved her body into a twist. It felt great! She twirled into an Axel and landed easily. Leaping upwards again, she tried the double toe loop.

She completed the move. But when she landed on the ice, she knew straight away that her footing was off.

Instead of landing cleanly, her ankle buckled.

Maggie closed her eyes as the ice flew towards her face.

Chapter Five

Marvellous!

"Maggie!" Shannon yelled from across the rink.

Maggie slowly sat up on the ice.

"Maggie! Are you all right?" Mr Peters asked. He slid over the ice in his trainers. He leaned down to help her up.

"Yes, I'm fine," Maggie said. "I'm not hurt." She brushed off invisible pieces of ice from her legs.

Her legs wobbled for a second as she stood up. "How embarrassing!" was all she could think.

"I guess I'm not ready for the junior level after all," Maggie said to her instructor.

Shannon, walking up to the nearest rail, frowned. "The junior level?" she exclaimed. "But you just got to novice! Mr Peters, seriously, tell her she's not ready for the junior level."

"Actually, I was the one who suggested it," Mr Peters said.

Shannon frowned and said, "Obviously, she's not ready."

"Maybe not," Mr Peters agreed. "But it doesn't hurt to try." He turned to Maggie. "Are you ready to skate?" he asked.

Maggie nodded. She skated away from Shannon and Mr Peters.

She shook her arms and rolled her head. She needed to shake off the feeling of falling. She'd fallen plenty of times while learning to skate.

Falling was never fun. The only cure for falling was getting back up again.

Maggie sped up as she skated around the rink. She pushed all thoughts of Shannon, Mr Peters, and falling from her mind. She focused only on moving her legs and soaring across the ice. She waved her arms gently behind her, like the wings of a bird.

The melody of Beethoven's *Moonlight Sonata* washed over her. She thought about watching her sister skate the day before.

Spinning, Maggie began to skate backwards. She lifted her arms above her head, just as Shannon had done. She tried to use her arms and hands with grace, like her ballet instructor had shown her.

Still skating backwards, Maggie suddenly wanted to jump. She wanted to leap up and twist through the air. She couldn't just skate. She had to do something else.

She threw her body upwards. She brought her arms in. She spun tightly in mid-air. Then she landed on the ice, her arms once again outstretched.

"Marvellous, Maggie!" shouted Mr Peters. "Just marvellous!"

For once, Maggie had to agree with him.

Chapter Six

Two Weeks to Go

A few days later, Elly and Maggie walked out of the rink together after skating practice. "Come on, let's go to town or something," Elly said. "You've been practising so much."

"I can't," Maggie said. "I have to practise more after dinner. And I still have to finish up that social studies project."

"The competition is two weeks away," Elly said. "You have plenty of time to practise."

Maggie hadn't told anyone that she was practising two different routines.

She worked on one routine with Mr Peters. That one was safe. She could skate it in her sleep. It had the right amount of jumps and spins for her level. The routine would earn her a good score in the competition.

Maggie wanted more than good. She wanted amazing. She wanted to outshine all the other skaters. So she had talked her parents into letting her skate one more hour every night.

Every night, alone at the rink, she listened to Beethoven's *Moonlight Sonata*. Only then, she skated the routine she would show to the judges.

"Come on, you can take one night off," Elly said.

"Sorry, I just can't," Maggie told Elly.

"Okay," Elly said sadly. "Maybe another time."

"See you tomorrow," Maggie said. She hurried home. She quickly finished her homework. Then she ate a light dinner with her family.

She couldn't wait to get back on the ice. She couldn't wait to finally practise her real routine.

"I think I'll go with you tonight," Shannon said after dinner. She stood at the kitchen sink. She rinsed off her plate and put it in the dishwasher.

Maggie brought her own plate to the sink. "Why would you want to do that?" she asked nervously. "You don't need extra practice."

Shannon shrugged. "I'm not doing anything tonight. And I can always use extra practice," she said.

Maggie gritted her teeth. How could she keep her routine a secret if Shannon went with her?

"Besides," Shannon went on, "Mr Peters and I have been working on my routine. It's going to be really great. He loved my music choice. I'd like to see what you think about it."

Maggie couldn't come up with a reason for Shannon not to go to the rink. "Fine," Maggie said. "I'd love to see your new routine."

"Great!" Shannon said. She smiled. She dried her hands on a tea towel and tossed it to Maggie.

"Yeah. Great," Maggie said, pretending to smile. She and Shannon finished cleaning up. Then they gathered their skating gear and headed to the rink.

Maggie decided she'd just practise her boring, easy routine. Just for one night.

At the rink, she tried to ignore Shannon, but she couldn't. She couldn't stop comparing her own skating style with Shannon's.

Shannon always scored really high during competitions. Her body seemed as if it were made for ice skating. Maggie always scored okay, but she never did as well as she wanted to.

This time, Maggie wanted it to be different. She knew she'd finally be the one to shine.

As Maggie laced up her skates, she saw Shannon put a CD into the skating rink's sound system. Suddenly, a familiar melody drifted from the speakers.

It was a melody Maggie knew well. It was her song.

It was Beethoven's *Moonlight Sonata*.

Chapter Seven

Another Song

Shannon came skating up.

"What are you doing?" Maggie asked her sister.

Shannon frowned. "What do you mean?" she asked. "I'm getting ready to skate, just like you."

"What are you doing with this song?" Maggie asked angrily.

Shannon smiled. "It's great, isn't it?" she said. "It's Beethoven's *Moonlight Sonata*."

"I know what song it is!" Maggie said.

"It's the song Mr Peters and I chose for my routine," Shannon said.

Maggie's jaw dropped. "Your routine?" she asked.

She knew she couldn't argue. She'd kept her song choice a secret. No one knew she planned to skate to the *Moonlight Sonata*.

Maggie swallowed. Then she asked, "How did you choose this song?"

"I heard it one day at the ballet studio," Shannon told her. "I hummed a few notes to Mr Peters, and he knew the song."

"The ballet studio," Maggie repeated.

"Actually, it was that day you thought you saw someone you knew in some other class," Shannon said.

She smiled. "I've been meaning to thank you," Shannon went on. "If you hadn't made us wait, I wouldn't have heard the song."

"You're welcome," Maggie muttered.

Shannon asked, "Do you want to watch my routine?"

That was the last thing Maggie wanted to do. No way did she want to compare Shannon's routine with her own. She knew it would make her feel terrible.

Maggie felt a lump rise in her throat. She'd have to watch Shannon skate. She'd have to watch as, once again, Shannon did better than her.

She couldn't accuse Shannon of stealing her song. After all, Shannon didn't know it was the song Maggie had chosen.

Maggie nodded. She was afraid that if she opened her mouth, she'd start crying. And crying was not something she did every day.

"The song's already started, so I'll start in the middle," Shannon said.

Maggie watched as her older, taller, more glamorous sister took off across the ice. Maggie moved over to the rail and leaned against it. She watched Shannon glide and float.

Shannon's arms waved like feathers above her head. She arched her back and went into a spin. She didn't make one mistake.

Finally, she completed her routine. The last chords of the *Moonlight Sonata* echoed through the skating rink.

Shannon skated up to Maggie and stopped. When she'd caught her breath, Shannon asked, "What do you think?"

"It was beautiful, Shannon," Maggie said. She meant it, too. Shannon was born to ice skate. She had an inner grace that was hard to ignore.

Maggie looked down. She didn't want to skate anymore. The routine she'd been so excited about now seemed so basic and boring.

Shannon threw her arm around her sister. "Your routine is pretty great, too," she said. "We're going to rock the competition!"

Maggie smiled weakly. Yeah, she'd rock it – but first, she'd have to find another song to skate to.

 # Heart for Skating

Mr Peters clapped his hands. "No, Maggie!" he shouted. "You're going the wrong way!"

Maggie heard his voice above the slither of her skates on the ice. He sounded a lot like Mrs Harris, her ballet teacher. Why did everyone seem to be yelling at her these days?

Maggie changed direction. She began to spin.

She bent her knees and went into a crouch. Then she pushed herself upwards. She continued to spin, her arms raised above her head. She stopped and threw her head back. The final spin was the end of her routine.

Maggie blew out a deep breath. Wiping sweat from her brow, she skated over to Mr Peters.

"Maggie, that was good," Mr Peters said. "But it wasn't great. I know you can do better."

Maggie breathed deeply. "I know," she said quietly. "I'll work harder."

Mr Peters sighed. He said, "I don't think it's how hard you work, Maggie. It's something else. It's like your heart isn't in the routine."

Maggie reached for her bottle of water. She unscrewed the cap and took a sip. "What do you mean?" she asked.

Mr Peters scratched his chin. "You're not skating with joy, like you used to. You're doing everything right, but something's missing," he said.

Maggie didn't know how to explain how she felt. Plenty of kids had problems with their brothers or sisters. She was no different. She had to find a way to get over feeling so bad when Shannon was around.

Mr Peters shook his head. "Think about what you love about skating. Listen to your heart as you skate, not to your head."

"Okay," Maggie said. "I'll try."

"Go skate," Mr Peters said. "Give it a try now."

Maggie skated and skated around the rink until she felt the rhythm of her movements. The ice was smooth beneath her skates. The air felt brisk against her cheeks. Everything smelled better when she skated.

With no music playing, her legs seemed to be moving in time to their own beat. Suddenly, Maggie thought of a song. It wasn't classical. It wasn't pop. But it brought a smile to Maggie's face.

She'd have to check with Mr Peters, but Maggie thought she'd finally found her song. In fact, maybe she'd finally found her heart for skating again.

Chapter Nine

Lost Balance

At the rink ten days later, Maggie tugged at a corner of her skating skirt. Her outfit was purple, her favourite colour. Small beads glittered across the body and on to the skirt. Maggie felt like an ice fairy when she wore it. She felt like she could skate better than anyone, even her sister.

"Hey!" Elly shouted, running over.

"Hey yourself!" Maggie called back. "Are you ready?"

"As ready as I'll ever be," Elly said. "Why am I so nervous? It's not like we haven't practised a squillion hours."

"I know," Maggie said. "But this is what all the lessons and practice and rink time are all about. Today, though, I just want to do better than Shannon."

Elly sat down on a bench. She leaned over and tightened up her laces. "I don't understand this jealousy you have with your sister," she said.

Maggie sat down next to her and asked, "Don't you ever feel competitive with your brothers?"

"I guess, sometimes," Elly said.

"Well, that's how I feel about Shannon," Maggie explained. "Just once I'd like to be better than she is at something."

Elly flung an arm around her friend's shoulder. "You silly thing! You're better at lots of things! You just don't see it."

Maggie felt herself blushing. Just then, the girls heard clapping coming from the rink.

"It sounds like Kathy Simmons just finished skating," Elly said.

"That means that Shannon is up next," Maggie said. "Let's go and watch."

Both girls wobbled to their feet. The blades of their skates were in plastic blade guards. Still, walking on the rubber mat wasn't exactly easy. Together, they stood in the entrance tunnel to the rink.

Shannon was already standing in the centre of the oval. Her arms were folded in front of her chest. Her head hung down.

Then the opening notes of Beethoven's Moonlight Sonata floated from the rink's speakers.

It was as if the music brought Shannon to life. Her arms unwound from her body. Suddenly she was sliding across the ice. Her movements were in perfect time to the music.

The music got louder. Maggie knew her sister was about to go into the hardest part of her routine. The crowd was quiet as everyone watched Shannon.

Maggie watched the routine carefully. Then, suddenly, Shannon lost her balance and stumbled on the ice.

 In the Zone

Maggie gasped. She'd never seen her sister stumble, not even in rehearsals.

Shannon continued to skate. Her stumble didn't stop her. In fact, Maggie thought her sister skated better than she ever had before.

Shannon skated off the ice, waving to the standing crowd. Maggie and Elly met Shannon at the exit. "What happened?" Maggie asked, taking Shannon's arm.

"I'm not sure," Shannon said. "I thought I had nailed that landing. I guess I was too confident."

"You?" Maggie said, smiling. "Too confident? Never!"

Shannon laughed. "Come sit with me while I wait for my scores," she said.

Maggie and Elly joined Shannon in the waiting area. Soon, the scores were announced. Shannon's average was 5.7 out of 6.0.

"That's pretty good, for someone who almost fell," Shannon said. She turned to Maggie and added, "Let's see if you can do better."

Maggie looked at her, surprised. "You know I try to beat your scores?" she asked quietly.

"Of course I do!" Shannon said, smiling. "What kind of sister would I be if there wasn't a little bit of healthy competition? Now, go out there and beat my 5.7!"

Without thinking about it, Maggie threw her arms around Shannon.

"I love you, Sis, even if you are perfect," Maggie said.

"Oh, stop!" Shannon said with a laugh. "Don't get all soppy on me! Now, go!"

Maggie skated to the middle of the rink. The cool air prickled across her skin. The ice felt smooth beneath her skates. She got into position for her routine.

Music burst from the speakers. The beat was sharp. Maggie tapped her skates to the rhythm. She pushed off across the ice, her body soaring with the music.

She'd chosen *All That Jazz*. The song was from one of her favourite musical shows, *Chicago*.

Maggie knew she was skating well. She felt powerful and sure of herself. She leaped and twirled and spun on the ice.

The music ended. Maggie waved to the crowd as she skated off the ice. Shannon was waiting for her. "That was incredible," Shannon said. "Let's go see your score."

"You won't be mad if it's higher than yours?" Maggie asked.

"Never!" Shannon said. "Don't you get it? Watching you skate makes me better."

Maggie put her arm through Shannon's. Together, they waited for Maggie's score.

When the judges announced that she'd scored 5.8, Shannon cheered louder than anyone else.

About the author

Lisa Trumbauer is the best-selling author of *A Practical Guide to Dragons*. In addition, she has written about 300 other books for children, including mystery novels, picture books, and non-fiction books on just about every topic under the sun (including the sun!).

About the illustrator

When Tuesday Mourning was a little girl, she knew she wanted to be an artist when she grew up. Now, she is an illustrator who especially loves working on books for children and teenagers. When she isn't illustrating, Tuesday loves spending time with her husband, who is an actor, and their son, Atticus.

Glossary

Axel   jump with a forwards take-off and 1½ rotations in the air

combination   two or more things put together

competition   contest

invisible   not able to be seen

jealousy   wanting something that someone else has

marvellous   wonderful

novice   lower level

rhythm   regular beat

routine   set way of doing a performance

studio   place where performers or dancers practise

stumble   trip

Famous female figure skaters

Over the years, there have been many famous and talented women skaters.

Sonja Henie was a figure skater from Norway in the 1920s and 30s. She won more Olympic and World titles than any other female figure skater. She went on to become one of the highest paid film stars in Hollywood.

Debi Thomas won a bronze medal in the 1988 Olympics. She was the first African American to win a figure-skating medal in the Olympics.

Midori Ito was the first woman to land a triple Axel during competition. She was also the first Asian woman to win a world figure-skating title. Ito won a silver medal in the 1992 Olympics.

Jayne Torvill is a British skater who won a gold medal in the 1984 Olympics and a bronze medal in the 1994 Olympics, with her skating partner Christopher Dean. They went on to present the popular TV programme *Dancing on Ice*.

At just 15 years old, Tara Lipinski became the youngest person to earn a gold medal in the winter Olympics. She won a gold medal in 1998.

Michelle Kwan has two Olympic medals, five World Championships, and nine US championships. Kwan is the most decorated figure skater in US history.

Discussion questions

1. Why is Maggie jealous of her sister? Do you think that Shannon is jealous of Maggie? Is it okay for siblings to be jealous of each other? Talk about your reasons.

2. Maggie keeps her song a secret from her coach and from her sister. Why did she do that? What do you think would have happened if she'd told her sister and coach about the *Moonlight Sonata*?

3. Maggie and Shannon are both figure skaters. Do you know any famous athletes, actors, writers, or musicians who are siblings?

Writing prompts

1. Maggie is jealous of her sister. Write about a time when you were jealous of someone. Who were you jealous of? Why were you jealous of them? What happened?

2. Maggie does well in the competition at the end of this book. What do you think happens next? Write a story that begins when this book ends.

3. Sometimes it's fun to think about a story from another person's point of view. Try writing chapter 10 from Shannon's point of view. What does she see and hear? What does she think and feel?

Nadia had an injury and couldn't
practise her balance beam routines all
summer. Now, every time she sees her rival
Claire, her ankle starts to hurt again. Will
Nadia let Claire's mean comments keep
her from winning?

New stables have opened up in town, and Molly convinces her parents to let her sign up for riding lessons. Everything is great, except that two girls at school keep making fun of her. How can Molly keep her confidence, both in and out of the saddle?

Find out more

Books

Skating School series, Linda Chapman
(Puffin, 2010)
Skate School: Ice Princess, Kay Woodward
(Usborne, 2009)

DVD

**Torvill & Dean's Dancing On Ice: The
Bolero 25th Anniversary Tour** (2009)
This DVD includes the ice dancing routine
that won Jayne Torvill and Christopher
Dean the gold medal at the Olympic
Games.

Website

http://www.olympic.org/uk/athletes
Do a search in the "Profiles" section to find
out more about Sonja Henie, Jayne Torvill,
and other figure skaters.